Celtic
TALES & LEGENDS

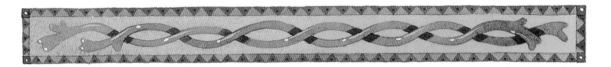

Introduction

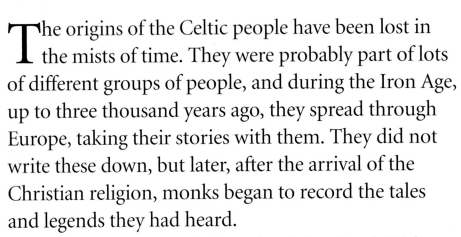

The origins of the Celtic people have been lost in the mists of time. They were probably part of lots of different groups of people, and during the Iron Age, up to three thousand years ago, they spread through Europe, taking their stories with them. They did not write these down, but later, after the arrival of the Christian religion, monks began to record the tales and legends they had heard.

Today, many people in Ireland, Scotland, Wales and parts of Britain and France think of themselves as Celts. And, of course, in the last three centuries, many Celtic people have continued to travel, settling in the United States, Canada, Australia and New Zealand.

So the stories of the Celts, with their descriptions of gorgeous clothes and jewels, fine cattle and heroic deeds, are still spreading across the world.

One of the stories in this book features a tiny magical man called a leprechaun, but he seems to have hopped onto other pages, too. Can you find him?

Celtic
TALES & LEGENDS

TEN MYSTICAL STORIES
RETOLD FOR CHILDREN

Illustrated by
CATHIE SHUTTLEWORTH

ARMADILLO

This edition is published by Armadillo, an imprint of Anness Publishing Ltd,
Blaby Road, Wigston, Leicestershire LE18 4SE; info@anness.com

www.annesspublishing.com

If you like the images in this book and would like to investigate using them for publishing, promotions
or advertising, please visit our website www.practicalpictures.com for more information.

Publisher: Joanna Lorenz
Designed by Amanda Hawkes
Editorial Consultant: Ronne Randall
Produced for Anness Publishing Ltd by Nicola Baxter
Senior Production Controller: Don Campaniello

A CIP catalogue record for this book is available from the British Library.

PUBLISHER'S NOTE
The author and publishers have made every effort to ensure that this book is safe for its intended use,
and cannot accept any legal responsibility or liability for any harm or injury arising from misuse.

Manufacturer: Anness Publishing Ltd, Blaby Road, Wigston, Leicestershire LE18 4SE, England
For Product Tracking go to: www.annesspublishing.com/tracking
Batch: 6066-20947-1127

Contents

Cormac's Golden Cup

When Cormac the High King looked out from the walls of his castle one day, he saw a warrior striding toward him through the green fields of corn. The man was dressed as a prince or king, in gold and purple brocade, and his crimson cloak had a golden yellow lining.

As he drew closer, the king saw that he was carrying a silver branch, from which hung three golden apples. As the warrior walked, the apples made a kind of music. It was the sort of sound that could ease old wounds and bring peaceful sleep.

As he drew near the castle, the warrior greeted the king with respect.

"I come," he said,
"from a land where no
lie is ever spoken, where
nothing grows old or
feeble, where there is no
sadness or envy or hate."

"Then you are
welcome indeed to my
court," replied the king.

The two men clasped wrists in greeting and at
once swore friendship. As the host, the king was
entitled to ask for a gift. Of course, he asked for the
silver branch with the golden apples. The stranger
gave it at once and chose three wishes in return – but
before he could claim them, he disappeared.

As Cormac walked back into his stronghold, the
golden apples made their music. At once, everyone in
the castle fell asleep.

Exactly a year and a day later, on a May morning, the warrior appeared again before Cormac the High King. This time his clothes were striped in pink and red like the rising and setting sun.

"I can guess why you are here," said Cormac, glad to see his noble visitor.

"Yes, I have come to claim the first of my wishes," replied the stranger. "I request the hand of your daughter in marriage."

Cormac was happy to agree, and when there were protests from the women of the court that they knew nothing of this stranger, the king simply shook the silver branch and sent them to sleep.

Another month passed, and again the stranger returned. This time he was dressed in deep sea-blue and the white of soft clouds.

"My second wish," he said, "is that you give me your young son to raise."

"Gladly," replied Cormac, and when the women, who loved the boy, complained, he sent them to sleep again with the silver branch.

It was a year and a day later that the stranger appeared for the fourth time. He was dressed in green and yellow, like the young corn and the bright sun.

"My final wish," he said, "is that you give me your wife."

Cormac would not break a promise, but his heart was torn as the warrior led his beloved wife away.

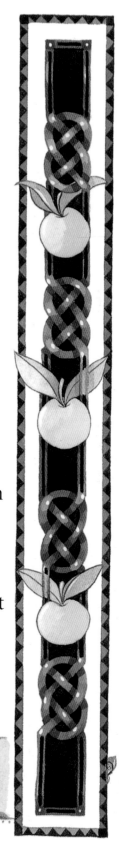

All at once, Cormac could bear it no more. He called his own warriors and set off after the pair. As the pursuing party left the castle far behind, a mist blew up from the sea. Cormac lost his companions and found himself alone on a desolate moor.

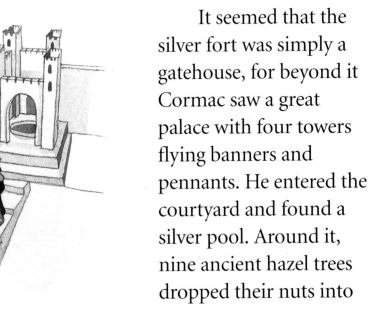

Suddenly, in front of him, a fort appeared, with gleaming silver walls. The door swung open as he approached. Inside, everything was silver, but high above men were trying to thatch the roof with white feathers that floated in the breeze.

It seemed that the silver fort was simply a gatehouse, for beyond it Cormac saw a great palace with four towers flying banners and pennants. He entered the courtyard and found a silver pool. Around it, nine ancient hazel trees dropped their nuts into the water, where five salmon snapped them up. Five streams flowed with tinkling music from the pool.

Inside the palace a beautiful woman and a knight were sitting on chairs of oak. Then a third man arrived, carrying a pig. He killed the pig and cut it into four, throwing it into a bubbling cauldron.

"Ah me," he sighed, "this pig will never be cooked until four true tales are told."

So the man himself told a story. The beautiful woman told another, followed by the knight. They turned to look at Cormac.

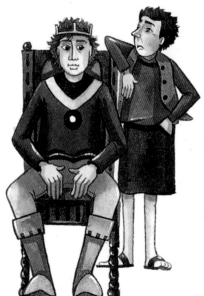

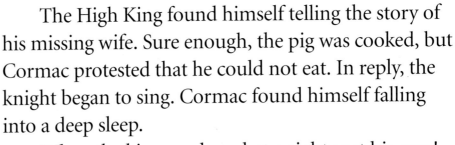

The High King found himself telling the story of his missing wife. Sure enough, the pig was cooked, but Cormac protested that he could not eat. In reply, the knight began to sing. Cormac found himself falling into a deep sleep.

When the king awoke, what a sight met his eyes! Fifty warriors attended him, and in their midst stood his wife, his daughter and his son.

How happy Cormac was! The hall was filled with music as they feasted together.

Polite as ever, the High King complimented his host on the beautiful golden goblet from which he drank.

"Ah," said the knight, "this is a magical cup. If three lies are told, it breaks into three parts. If three truths are told, it is made whole again."

The knight duly told three lies, and the goblet shattered. Then he said, "No man has touched your wife or daughter. No woman has been near your son." At once, the cup became whole again. It was the knight's way of showing that Cormac's family had been kept safe.

The High King showed his astonishment.

"It is simple," replied his host. "I am Manannan MacLir, god of the sea. I brought you here to show you the Promised Land."

Suddenly it became clear to Cormac that this was none other than the warrior who had visited his castle.

"I will give you this golden goblet," said his host, "to go with the silver branch with the golden apples."

Then Manannan explained the meaning of the strange things that Cormac had seen. The pool in the courtyard was the source of knowledge. The streams that flowed from it were the sense of sight, hearing, smell, taste and touch, which bring knowledge into our souls. The white feathers were wealth, which it is foolish to try to chase, as it blows away as lightly as a feather.

At last the whole company bowed to the High King, and left him to sleep.

When Cormac awoke the next morning, he found himself back in his stronghold of Tara. He could see his people going about their business as usual, with his wife, his daughter and his son among them. Perhaps it had all been a dream.

Then the king noticed two things. Gleaming in the morning sun stood a golden goblet and a silver branch, with little golden apples on it.

Deirdre of the Sorrows

Long ago, in the days of King Conor MacNessa of Ulster, a girl was born who was extraordinarily beautiful. She had shining, golden hair, misty green eyes, and lips as red as cherries. Her name was Deirdre, and her fate was not to be an ordinary one.

Before Deirdre was born, it was prophesied that she would bring great trouble to Ulster. Many fine men, it was said, would die because of her beauty.

Knowing of the prophecy, King Conor decided to take charge of the girl's upbringing himself. He sent her to a remote castle in the middle of a forest, where no man would see her beauty and lose his senses because of it. He even planned to marry her himself, to try to avoid the trouble that had been foretold.

It was not to be.

As Deirdre grew older and ever more lovely, the King visited her often. He looked forward to the day when he could make her his wife. Deirdre was not so sure. She asked her nurse if all men were as old and withered as King Conor. The nurse had to confess that they were not. Wishing the girl a happier fate than to marry a man more than twice her age, she helped her to meet a young warrior by the name of Naoise.

Dark-haired Naoise, glowing with health, was as handsome as Deirdre was beautiful. The two young people fell rapidly in love. Fearing the King's anger, Naoise asked his two brothers, Ardan and Ainle, to help him carry Deirdre away. It was several days before King Conor discovered they had gone.

Then the King's anger was frightening to see. He set off after the couple with his mightiest warriors, his speediest horses and his keenest hounds. For years, the fugitives were pursued through the length and breadth of Ireland.

At last, just as it seemed they must be caught, the four took a boat to Scotland. There, safe from King Conor's reach, the three brothers gained almost as much power and renown as they had known in their much-missed homeland.

Years passed. The bitterness in King Conor's heart did not lessen, but when men he respected suggested that it was time he showed his greatness by pardoning the runaways, he agreed.

It took a long time to persuade Naoise and his brothers that it was safe for them to return. At last, Deirdre, Naoise, Ardan and Ainle found themselves on Irish soil once more. As they approached King Conor's castle, Deirdre suddenly cried out. She had a terrible fear that her husband was in danger.

She was right. The King was determined to take his revenge on the warriors who had humiliated him. Deirdre was seized and dragged, screaming, into his castle. By the end of the day, her husband and his brothers were dead, and many another noble warrior lay where he had fallen.

It was a hollow victory. Although Deirdre lived with King Conor for a year and a day, she refused to speak or look at him. She was as beautiful as ever, but there was no happiness for her royal husband.

At last, the King could bear it no longer. He ordered his charioteer to take Deirdre away. But the heartbroken girl threw herself from the chariot. Deirdre of the Sorrows, as she had come to be known, was no more.

It is said that from the graves of Deirdre and Naoise, two stately yew trees grew. Their branches stretched and spread, until they touched at last, as if uniting the lovers whose fate had been so sad.

The Land of Youth

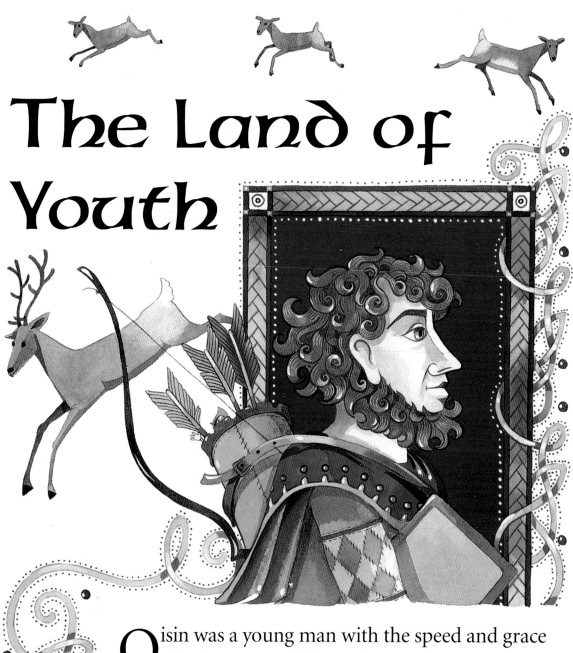

Oisin was a young man with the speed and grace of a deer. He could run faster, jump higher and hunt more cunningly than any of his companions. And he was a fine poet.

One day, when out hunting, green-eyed Oisin found himself in a place where thick woods and great mountains stretched down to the shores of a lake. The sight that met his eyes filled him with astonishment.

A figure was riding toward the young man on a white horse shod with silver. The horse was strong and spirited, the rider small and dainty, but she rode with great skill … across the shining water!

As she grew nearer, Oisin could see that the rider wore a dark red cloak, covered with golden stars. Around the border, flowers and honeybees were embroidered. The woman had deep, red-gold hair with a small white crown upon it. With her dark eyes, she did not seem Irish at all.

The white horse sported a golden plume. As Oisin watched, the woman expertly rode the beast out of the water and up the rough ground toward him.

"My name is Niav of the Golden Hair," she said. "I come from a wonderful land where flowers always bloom and fruit hangs ripe on the trees. There is no pain there. No illness. No death. And no one grows old. It is the Land of Youth."

Oisin's companions seemed to be in a trance. No one moved as Niav went on. "I have been searching for you for seven years," she told Oisin. "My father, who rules the Land of Youth, has allowed me to come for you. Will you go with me?"

"Lady, I will," replied Oisin. "I am yours forever."

He slipped onto the back of her horse and rode with her, out across the lake in a gleam of light, with drops of spray glittering in the air around them.

On and on rode Oisin and Niav, along a fast-flowing river. Gradually, the river widened and high cliffs appeared on either side. Fearlessly, Niav rode out into the sea, her horse galloping sure-footedly over the waves.

"Look!" cried Niav, and ahead the sea mist cleared to reveal a golden land rising from the waters. It was just as Niav had described it. In the distance, a great round castle shone in the sunhine, with seven banners in the shades of the rainbow fluttering from its walls. Outside the castle, a crowd of people had gathered to greet Oisin. Everyone was smiling.

"These people will serve you," Niav told her chosen husband, "from the moment your foot touches the ground. But you can never return to your homeland after that, for there is no time in the Land of Youth. If you ever leave, all the years that you have spent here will fall upon you."

"I have given my word to remain with you," said Oisin, "and I will keep it." With that, he leaped to the ground. As he did so, he seemed to become taller, fairer and sturdier, while his skin darkened so that he looked more like Niav. At the same time, his rough hunting clothes became a blue silk tunic and a golden cloak.

Oisin looked around with pleasure. As far as the eye could see, orchards heavy with fruit stretched around the castle, bearing lemons, cherries and plump peaches.

"Beyond those hills," said Niav, "are the farms where our people grow dreams. Beyond those mountains is the Land of Silence, where those who wish can sit in peace and watch the patterns of the light and the sky."

After the wedding of Niav and Oisin, Niav's father the King journeyed to the Land of Silence, and the young people ruled in his place. Those were golden years. Who knows how many of them passed? But slowly, Oisin became less and less satisfied with his ideal life. He longed to return to his homeland – if only for a day.

Against her better judgment, Niav lent Oisin her white horse so that he could return just once to the land of his birth.

"But remember," she said, "while you are there you must not set your foot upon the ground. If you do so, the years you have spent here will fall around you and you can never return to the Land of Youth."

Oisin's heart was full as he set off across the sea. His horse galloped swiftly over the waves until he came to the shores of Ireland. But although the young man rode the length and breadth of the country, he could find no one that he recognized. Even the people working in the fields seemed different and spoke a language he could barely understand.

The ramparts of his castle were overgrown with grass. When he called the names of his companions, none came. By a cliffside, he came across some men and managed to explain to them that he was Oisin, son of Finn MacCool.

The men were astonished. Oisin, they said, had lived hundreds of years before and was part of ancient legend now.

Oisin was appalled. He set his horse at a gallop along the beach, but as he did so, the girth broke and he found himself falling to the sand. As he touched the soil of Ireland, he began to change. His skin wrinkled and grew ashen. His clothes fell to dust. His eyes misted over. In a second, Oisin became an ancient man, several hundred years old.

It was at this time that Saint Patrick was wandering through Ireland. He tended to the feeble man, writing down his stories of days long ago. Then Oisin died, and the age of heroes died with him.

Bran and Branwen

Insults can hurt as much as wounds, and they can be as hard to heal. The mighty King Bran found this to his cost.

Now Bran was a great man in more ways than one. As well as being a powerful ruler, he was also so large that no house had ever been built to fit him.

One day, Bran was sitting by the Welsh coast with his court when he saw thirteen fine ships sailing toward him. A small boat was lowered from the leading ship, and a messenger rowed ashore.

"I am sent," he said, "from Lord Mattholoch of Ireland, who comes in peace to make a most important request of you."

It seemed that the Irish lord wanted to marry King Bran's sister, whose name was Branwen.

Bran called his advisers and discussed the matter. Lord Mattholoch would be a powerful friend to have. The marriage seemed a good idea.

So Bran ordered a great wedding feast to be prepared, and it was set up in enormous tents, as no building could accommodate the king.

But before the feast could take place, Bran's half-brother, called Evnissien, returned. He was furious that important agreements had been made in his absence and, looking for a way to hurt Bran, he killed the horses of the Irishmen – and in a horrible way.

Bran knew nothing of this. The first sign of a problem was when it was reported to him that the Irish were heading for their ships – without the marriage taking place.

After that, it was not long before Bran heard of Evnissien's dreadful act. He was appalled. The Irish, who would make such good allies, would now be powerful enemies. King Bran sent messengers after Lord Mattholoch to beg him to return. He offered to replace all the horses and give many gifts besides.

Reluctantly, Lord Mattholoch agreed, but the wedding feast was a rather subdued affair. In an effort to improve matters, King Bran gave one more great gift – a magic cauldron. If a soldier killed in battle was thrown into it, he would come back to life again, although he would no longer be able to speak.

Lord Mattholoch seemed very pleased with all his gifts and willing to let bygones be bygones. He sailed to Ireland with his new bride and many promises of friendship.

But back at home, although Branwen was a much-loved queen and soon gave birth to a son, Lord Mattholoch couldn't help thinking about the insult that had been done to him in Wales. His courtiers pointed out that he had never taken revenge. Poor Branwen was the only one of the Welsh that Lord Mattholoch could reach. He banished her from his side and sent her to work in the palace kitchens. All contact between Ireland and Wales was cut off, so that King Bran would not find out about his sister's fate.

For three years, Branwen lived a miserable life. The only friendship she had was that of a little starling, who came and perched on the windowsill and sang to her of fresh air and freedom. One day, Branwen tied a message to the starling's leg and sent it eastward, hoping that it might carry news of her to her brother.

The starling did its duty well. When he read of his sister's treatment, King Bran was overwhelmed with feelings of sorrow and rage. At once, he ordered his armies to make ready.

When Bran's massive fleet set sail for Ireland, with
the huge king wading through the water at its head,
the masts of the ships appeared to those on the Irish
shore like a massive forest moving across the sea. Only
Branwen guessed what was happening. She dreaded
the fighting that must surely follow and begged her
husband to try to make peace with Bran.

A big gesture was
needed, and Mattholoch
made it. He announced
that he was making his
young son, Branwen's
child, lord of all his lands.
In addition, he said, he
would build King Bran a
house – the first he had
ever had.

The house, when finished, was indeed fine, but Mattholoch's men laid a trap in every room. From each pillar hung a great bag. Bran was told that these contained flour and other goods, but an armed soldier hid in every one. Once again, Bran's half-brother Evnissien played a part in the drama. He discovered the treachery and dealt with it in his own fashion.

But violence breeds violence. That night, feeling he was in a world where nothing could be trusted, Evnissien killed the innocent boy who was about to be made ruler. At once, fighting – worse than anything Branwen had feared – broke out.

In the thick of the battle, Bran protected his sister, but the Welsh had the worst of it, especially when Lord Mattholoch began to use the magic cauldron that Bran had given him all those years before. Then, once more, Evnissien played a vital part. He broke the cauldron and gave the advantage once more to Bran's men.

At last, with only seven men remaining, Bran and Branwen set off for home, leaving Ireland devastated behind them. But Bran had been wounded. He died before he left Irish soil. Branwen herself did reach Wales, but her heart was broken. She did not live to mourn her brother.

Between Wales and Ireland, the ceaseless waves rolled as before. It was many years before they washed away the harm that was done the day that thirteen ships sailed upon them.

The Three Troubles

King Llud of Britain and his brother Llewelys were very close. They helped each other out in times of trouble. When the King of France died, Llewelys heard that his only child was a daughter – an unmarried one. After consulting with his brother, Llewelys set out to win the princess. Before long, the brothers were both rulers – of Britain and of France.

But Llud soon found himself in difficulty. Three great troubles came to plague his peaceful country.

First of all, there were the Coroniads, who arrived from a foreign country. These strange people were soon able to do anything they liked, for they used powerful magic and could overhear any conversation anywhere in the country. It was useless to try to plot against them. They always knew what the plans were.

The second of Llud's troubles came only once a year, on the night before May Day, but it unnerved the whole country. It was a scream. You might not think that this was such a dreadful thing, but it was the kind of scream that made blood run cold and milk curdle. Grown men trembled for weeks afterward.

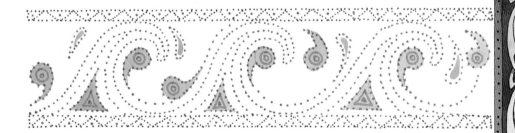

The third trouble was even more serious. All kings, especially wise ones like Llud, like to store up supplies to stand by them in difficult times. Yet every night, every storeroom in the country, even in Llud's own palace, was emptied. It was extremely worrying.

Llud tried everything he could think of to improve matters in his country, but it was no use. At last, he set sail for France to consult his brother.

Llewelys, hearing of Llud's approach, sailed out to meet him. Their two ships met in the middle of the sea, apart from their following fleets.

The first problem was to prevent the Coroniads from overhearing the conversation. Llewelys had an answer for that. He ordered a long, long hunting horn to be made of bronze. It stretched between the two ships and could be held so closely to the speaker's mouth and the listener's ear that the Coroniads could hear nothing.

When Llewelys understood Llud's difficulties, he was able to see the problems as an outsider.

"The Coroniads can be defeated," he said, "by means of a special potion. I will give you the recipe. As for the dreadful scream, it is clear to me that this is the work of a dragon, fighting with another dragon above your kingdom. You must dig a great pit and stay up yourself on May Day Eve to capture them."

"And the missing stores?" asked Llud. "That is what troubles me most of all."

"Clearly, this is the work of a powerful wizard," said Llewelys. "You will have to fight him when he comes at night, after everyone has fallen asleep. The important thing is not to fall asleep yourself. I have an idea about that, too."

So Llud thanked his brother and returned to his own land. At once, he began, without telling a soul, to make the potion his brother had told him about. Then he ordered that the potion should be sprinkled on every man, woman and child in the country. His own people did not feel a thing, but the Coroniads dropped like flies. They would be no more trouble.

No sooner had Llud solved this problem than May Day approached. Llud had an enormous pit dug in the very middle of the country. Then he himself took up his position near it and waited.

Night fell. High above him in the heavens, the terrible scream rang out. Llud almost collapsed with fright, but he remembered Llewelys's words and stood firm. Sure enough, two dragons could be seen fighting above him.

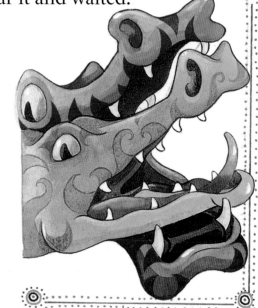

All night they fought, until as dawn began to brighten the sky, they seemed to have shrunk to the size of two little pigs. Quickly, Llud caught the pigs in his pit and shut them up in a stone casket. The awesome scream was never heard again.

Now only one trouble remained, and Llud prepared himself to deal with it. He had a huge barrel filled with ice-cold water and placed beside his chair. Then he invited everyone who was anyone to a great feast in his palace.

All evening, food was piled high on huge tables and mead flowed freely. As midnight approached, Llud's guests could hardly move – filled with food or drink … or both! One by one, their heads drooped and they fell asleep where they sat.

Llud felt pretty sleepy, too. His eyes began to close and his goblet slipped from his grasp. But just in time, he jumped into the barrel of cold water. It's hard to sleep when your teeth are chattering and your knees are knocking!

Llud did not have long to wait. Soon after midnight, an imposing figure came into the hall. He looked like a warrior, but he was clearly a wizard, for he quickly began gathering up all the food and drink into a basket. No matter how much he put in, the basket was never full. When every scrap of bread, meat and mead in the place had been gathered up, the stranger left the hall.

Then Llud leaped out of his barrel and ran after the wizard, warmed by indignation and waving his sword. The wizard proved to be a valiant fighter. Backwards and forwards the two men fought. Sparks jumped from their clashing swords. Llud's powers were tested to their limits, but he overcame the wizard at last.

"I will spare your life," he said, "if you return everything you have taken, tonight and every night, and promise never to bother my country again."

The wizard promised.

Once again, Llud ruled over a peaceful realm. He made London into a fine city, with walls and towers and rich houses. Some say the city was named after him. Others point to Ludgate Hill as proof that Llud really was once king of all he surveyed.

Elidore

Along time ago in Wales, in the days of St. David, a boy named Elidore went daily to a monastery to learn from the monks. But all the time that the good brothers were making him copy his letters and showing him the beautiful illuminated manuscripts they produced themselves, Elidore was gazing wistfully out of the tiny windows at the bright, green world beyond.

The monks were gentle at first, but they began to despair of their pupil and became stricter and stricter. It was no use. One day when he was twelve years old, Elidore ran away from the monastery and out into the great forest nearby.

Freedom! Elidore breathed the sweet air and ran among the mighty trees. For two days he wandered, eating only the fruits and berries of the forest.

At last, Elidore found himself in front of a cave near a sparkling stream. He flopped down on the bank and began to drink. Suddenly, he noticed two little men standing beside him. They had long hair and were perfectly proportioned, but they only came up to his knees!

"Come with us," said one of the little men, "and we will take you to a land where you can run and play all day."

This sounded good to Elidore. Without hesitation, he followed the little men into the cave, stooping and crawling to keep up with them. At the back of the cave was a long, dark passage, but Elidore went on and finally came out into the most wonderful land. It had woods, meadows, rivers and lakes, fresh and green on every side. The only strange thing was that the sun never shone by day and the moon was never seen by night. Thick clouds covered the sky all the time.

The little men took Elidore to visit their king, who was no bigger than they were.

"You can be my son's page," said the king.

So Elidore served the prince and enjoyed himself very much. The little people were kind and friendly. They didn't make him study or stay indoors. But as time passed, he began to find it strange to be the biggest person in the land – and, of course, he was still growing. More and more, Elidore longed to see some people of his own size.

When he could bear it no longer, Elidore went to the king and asked permission to return to the world of humans to visit his mother.

"Of course," said the king, "but you must promise me that you will come back to us."

Elidore promised.

One fine day, the little people led the boy back through the dark, cramped passage, out of the mouth of the cave, and through the forest to his mother's little cottage.

"My boy! My boy!" she cried, running out to greet him with tears in her eyes. The little people just seemed to melt away.

Naturally, Elidore's mother wanted to know where he had been. She could hardly believe it when he told her. Just as naturally, she wanted him to stay now that he was home again. But Elidore had made a promise to the king.

After a while, he went back to the cave and returned to the world of the little people. He made his mother promise that she wouldn't tell another soul where he was.

After that, Elidore visited his mother many times, but he always went back to the prince's side. Each time, his mother would ask him to tell her more about the strange place that she had never seen.

One day, when he was describing the wonderful games he played with the young prince, Elidore happened to mention that the balls they rolled and threw were made of yellow, shiny metal.

His mother's eyes widened.

"That sounds like gold to me," she said. "Just one of those balls would be worth a fortune in our world. Couldn't you … er … bring one of them back as a souvenir for your poor old mother?"

So it was that next time Elidore left the land of the little people, he picked up one of the golden balls and didn't wait for his friends to guide him to the dark passage. After all, he had used it so many times that he could find it by himself now.

This time, Elidore hurried on his way to his mother's house. He knew perfectly well that he was doing something wrong. And however fast he ran, he always thought he could hear little footsteps behind him, dodging through the trees, pattering down the lanes. At last, he saw his mother's cottage, and his mother on the doorstep to greet him.

But as Elidore reached his mother, in his haste he stumbled and fell full-length on the path. The golden ball rolled from his fingers.

At once, two little men rushed past his outstretched hand, scowling and spitting at him as they passed. They seized the golden ball and ran away, disappearing before Elidore could scramble to his feet.

Elidore felt ashamed. He stayed with his mother for longer this time, and although she was disappointed not to have the golden ball, she was pleased to see her son.

Maybe by now you will be getting the idea that for Elidore, the grass was always greener somewhere else. He found himself thinking more and more about the land of the little people. At last, he decided it was time to go back.

Back through the forest went Elidore. He found the sparkling stream. He found the grassy bank. But the cave was nowhere to be seen. For days he searched, but he never saw it again.

So Elidore found himself at the monastery once more. After many years of study, he became a monk himself. Yet it wasn't for his learning or his goodness that Elidore became famous. It was for his stories of the little folk. People came from far and wide to hear him speak of them.

And to the day he died, whenever Elidore spoke of those happy days, his eyes filled with tears.

The Fountain

One day at King Arthur's court, the warrior Cunon told a story. He described how, as a young man, he set off into the world in search of adventure.

Before long, Cunon came upon a fine castle, where he was greeted with great hospitality. Beautiful women brought him food and fresh clothes. He found himself eating from gold, silver and ivory dishes.

At last, Cunon's hosts asked him the purpose of his journey. The young warrior explained that he was looking for a man who could match him in battle.

"Then you must go back into the woods," he was told, "until you come to a clearing. There you will find a dark and mighty man with one eye in the middle of his forehead and one leg and broad foot under the middle of his body."

Cunon did as he was told, and when he found the giant, he explained what he was seeking.

"Make your way to the next valley," replied the giant, "and there you will see a huge, green tree. Beneath it is a fountain. A silver bowl, chained to a marble stone, lies nearby. Fill the bowl with water and pour it on the stone. Wonders will happen."

Once again, Cunon did exactly as he was told. As the water fell, the earth shook beneath his feet. A great rushing sound filled the air and huge, icy hailstones pelted down on him. Then, just as suddenly, all the birds of the air began to sing, and the warrior saw, riding toward him, a man dressed all in black.

Here at last was an opponent worthy of Cunon's skill. But no mighty battle took place. In seconds, the stranger had hurled Cunon from his horse and left him, humiliated, on the ground. Cunon returned to Arthur's court, his pride wounded.

Now, it so happened that a knight called Owen was one of those listening to Cunon's tale. While the others were still discussing it, he silently saddled his horse and rode away, determined to find the stranger in black.

Everything happened exactly as Cunon had described it, but this time, Owen proved himself the better soldier. The black knight, receiving a mighty blow, turned his horse and fled.

Hot on his heels, Owen rode after him, until the knight rode at speed across the drawbridge of a huge castle. Owen followed, but as he passed through the gates, the portcullis and the inner doorway fell, trapping him between them.

Owen was still wondering what to do when a girl in a yellow dress passed by. She told Owen that he was in great danger. Then she slipped a ring from her finger.

"As long as you hold this," she said, "you will be invisible."

Using the ring, Owen was able to escape into the castle, where the girl, whose name was Luned, fed him and bound up his wounds.

Later, as he sat with Luned in a richly decorated chamber, Owen heard terrible cries ringing through the castle. He hurried to the window and looked out.

Far below, lit by hundreds of candles, a funeral procession was taking place. The black knight had died.

But Owen had no thought of pity or regret. He had eyes only for the woman who followed the procession.

"She is a countess, the black knight's widow," explained Luned. She could see at once that Owen had fallen dreadfully in love with the lady. "I will do what I can for you," said Luned, although she herself was more than a little smitten by the young man.

Luned hurried to the countess. "In your grief, you cannot think straight," she said, "but you know that, with your husband dead, you must find another champion to protect you and the magic fountain. I will ride to the court of King Arthur to find such a man."

But Luned did not ride from the castle. Instead, she crept back to her chamber and gave Owen rich, golden robes to wear. Then she led him to the countess.

The black knight was only just dead, but the fountain needed protection and Owen was a very handsome man. It was not long before he became the husband of the beautiful countess.

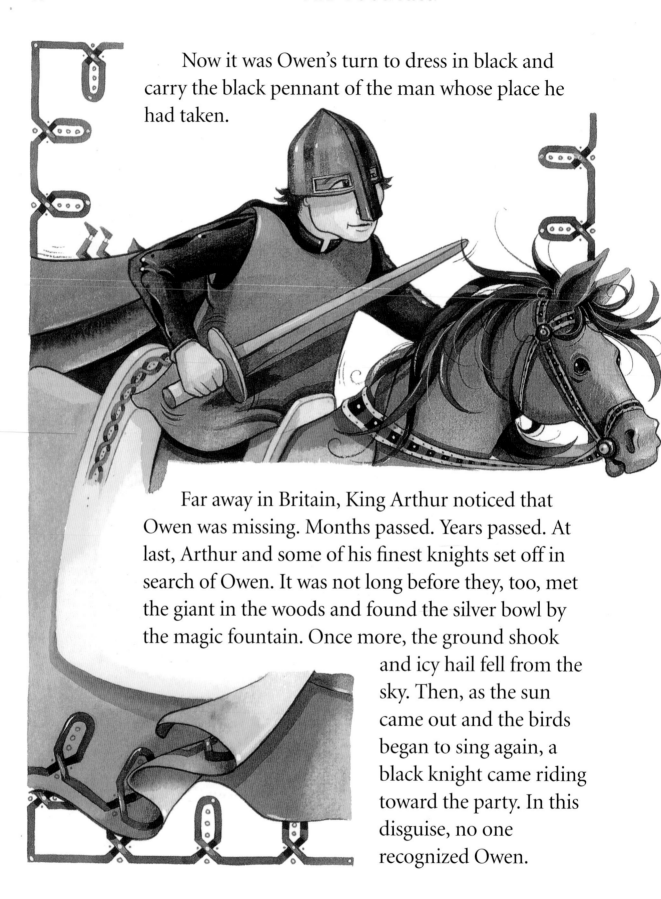

Now it was Owen's turn to dress in black and carry the black pennant of the man whose place he had taken.

Far away in Britain, King Arthur noticed that Owen was missing. Months passed. Years passed. At last, Arthur and some of his finest knights set off in search of Owen. It was not long before they, too, met the giant in the woods and found the silver bowl by the magic fountain. Once more, the ground shook and icy hail fell from the sky. Then, as the sun came out and the birds began to sing again, a black knight came riding toward the party. In this disguise, no one recognized Owen.

The fighting lasted for days. First one and then another of Arthur's finest champions challenged the black knight and fell. At last, when hardly any of Arthur's knights were left standing, a warrior named Gwalkmy begged to try his skill.

For three days the battle raged. At last both men were unseated from their horses and fought on foot. Then, with a mighty blow, Gwalkmy broke the black knight's helmet, revealing his face. At the same moment, Owen's sword smashed his opponent's visor. For the first time, each man saw his opponent face to face.

Of course, as soon as they recognized each other, the fighters threw down their arms. After a mighty feast, the countess gave Owen permission to return to King Arthur's court for three months.

Owen's adventures were far from over. But how his three months became three years, and how the lovely Luned gained her heart's desire at last, is another tale, and another must tell it.

The Two Pig-Keepers

You may have heard of the Great Cattle Raid of Ulster and the battles that followed it, but the story of how the famous bulls came to be born is less well known. This is what happened.

The King of Munster and the King of Connacht were great rivals, but their two pig-keepers, Friuch and Rucht, were friends. The two men would often drive their herds into each other's lands to eat acorns and beech nuts and grow fat. The pig-keepers had something else in common, too. They both performed magic and could change into any shape they liked.

Some people found it strange that the two men got on so well together. They did their best to create trouble between them by claiming that one or other of them was more powerful in magic.

The next time that the two pig-keepers met, they laughed about what was happening.

"They say you are more powerful than me," grinned Friuch.

"I wouldn't disagree," smiled his friend.

"Now I'm not so sure," Friuch replied. "Let's test it. I'll cast a spell over your pigs so that they don't get fat – however much they eat."

So that is what he did. Sure enough, Rucht's animals went home with him in a sorry state.

Although his friends mocked him, Rucht wasn't worried at all.

"Next time I take my pigs to his land, I'll cast the same spell on him," he said.

Sure enough, that is exactly what happened.

"Now it is clear that we are just as powerful as each other," said the two pig-keepers, looking at their skinny animals.

Of course, the kings of Connacht and Munster were not so happy. They dismissed their pig-keepers and employed two new ones who were interested in what pig-keepers should be interested in – making pigs fat!

Friuch and Rucht, however, stayed together. They took on the shape of birds of prey and sat together, first in one kingdom and then in the other, arguing and chattering all day long.

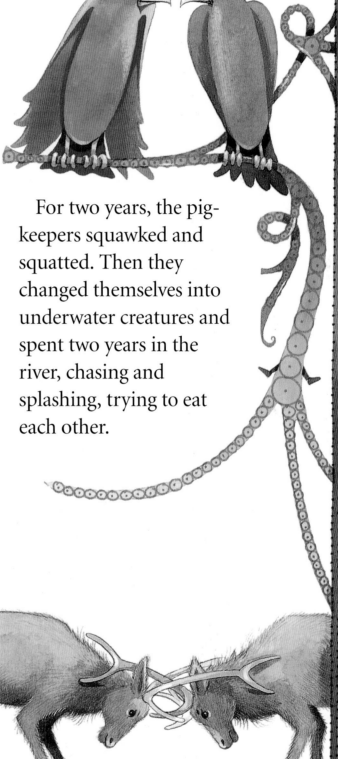

For two years, the pig-keepers squawked and squatted. Then they changed themselves into underwater creatures and spent two years in the river, chasing and splashing, trying to eat each other.

Next, the pig-keepers changed themselves into stags, trying to steal each other's does and stamping and trampling in the forests.

It didn't stop there. They became two warriors. The clash of their swords and their fearsome battle cries rang out over the land.

They became two phantoms, howling in the night, trying to frighten each other out of their wits.

The phantoms shimmered into dragons, roaring through the skies and bringing bad weather into the land, until it was knee-deep in snow.

At last, the dragons dropped to earth – as two, fat, maggoty worms. They squiggled into two springs and were drunk up by two cows. And, last of all, the cows gave birth to the finest bulls in the country, the Brown Bull of Cuailnge and the White Bull of Ai Plain. And these were the bulls that were the beginning of all the trouble to come.

Imagine a warm bed, covered with rich fabrics and furs. Surely this is not the place for trouble to start? But start it did when, late one night, King Ailill and Queen Maeve got to talking about their great possessions.

Both came from wealthy and powerful families. Both had brought to their marriage gold and silver, jewels and silks, sheep and cattle. And, they found, they were more or less evenly matched – until it came to looking in detail at the cattle. For King Ailill owned the White Bull of Ai Plain and Queen Maeve had nothing to match him.

Queen Maeve did not like to be beaten. She was particularly upset because the famous bull had once been her own. When she heard of the mighty Brown Bull of Cuailnge, she was determined to do everything she could to obtain it – which is what caused the Great Cattle Raid of Ulster and all that followed.

The Field of Gold

One sunny day at harvest-time, a lad was walking along a lane when he heard a strange tapping sound. He was surprised and peered into the hedge to see what it was.

Well, the cause of the sound was even more surprising. Among the roots of the hedge sat a very tiny old man, wearing a leather apron. He was hammering away at the heel of a little shoe, but every now and then he stood on tiptoe on his stool and drew himself a drink from a large brown barrel, half-hidden by the leaves.

"I've heard of leprechauns," the lad said to himself, "but I never really believed in them until today. If this one will lead me to his gold, I need never work again. I mustn't let him out of my sight."

Then the lad greeted the leprechaun as politely as he could, and the little old man nodded in a friendly way.

"I wonder if you'd be good enough to tell me what you are drinking?" asked the lad.

"It's beer," said the leprechaun, "and very fine beer, too."

"I'm sure it is," replied the lad, for the sun was making him thirsty. "Where did you find it?"

"Find it? I made it!" cried the shoemaker. "I made it from the purple heather."

The lad began to laugh. "You can't expect me to believe *that*," he roared. But still, he did want to taste the beer and said as much to the little man.

But the leprechaun looked severely at the young man and shook his head.

"You'd be better off minding your own business than bothering me," he said. "While you've been wasting time here, the cows have got into your father's wheat field and are trampling it all down."

The lad was just about to rush off to the wheat field when he remembered that this chance might not come his way again. He plunged into the hedge and grabbed the leprechaun, knocking over the beer as he did so.

Now, of course, there was no chance of a drink, and that made the young man even angrier. He shook the little old man in his fist and yelled, "If you don't show me where your gold is hidden, you won't live another minute."

"It's only a couple of fields away," squeaked the little man. "I'll show you."

So, with the lad holding fast to the leprechaun and never taking his eyes off him for a second, the strange pair made their way over hedges and ditches until they came to a great field of golden ragwort.

The leprechaun pointed to a particularly large and fine plant.

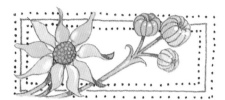

"That's where it is," he said. "If you dig under there, you'll find a pot full of golden coins."

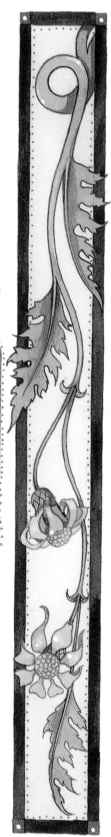

The lad was so delighted to hear this that it was a moment before he realized he did not have a spade with him. He would have to run home to fetch one. He pulled off his red neckerchief and tied it around the plant in question so that he would be able to find it again. But he was still suspicious.

"Promise me you won't untie that neckerchief," he said as fiercely as he could to the leprechaun.

The little man looked him straight in the eye and promised not to touch it.

"Will that be all, then?" he grinned.

The lad felt sure he had covered everything.

"It will," he said. "I've no more need of you. Goodbye and good luck!" And he set the little man down on the ground.

The leprechaun ran off at once. The young man could only just hear his last words.

"Good luck to you, too, my lad, in your field of gold. And much good may it do you!"

The foolish lad ran home as fast as he could and returned, panting, with his trusty spade. It was only minutes since he had said goodbye to the leprechaun. He was still much too late. Standing golden in the sun were thousands upon thousands of ragwort plants – and every one of them had a red neckerchief tied around it.

The lad walked slowly home, shaking his head. He had missed out on the beer. He had missed out on the gold. He had missed his chance altogether. And the language he used about that leprechaun was hardly fit to hear….

The Gift of Healing

There was once a shepherd who spent his days on the slopes of the Black Mountains of Wales. There, nestling between the hills, is a lake. Its waters are dark and still. Only the white clouds, floating above, move across them.

One fine day, as his sheep grazed peacefully around him, the shepherd sat down on the grass to rest. Suddenly, from out of the lake rose three beautiful maidens. The water dripped from their hair and clothes like crystal drops, glinting in the sun. It seemed as though they walked across the water itself to reach the shore.

The shepherd scrambled to his feet as one of the maidens moved gracefully toward him. The nearer she came, the more stunning did her beauty appear. The shepherd lost his heart to her in an instant. Desperately afraid that she might disappear as suddenly as she had come, he offered her the only thing he had – some bread from his knapsack.

The lovely girl took the bread and tasted it. Then, laughing, she handed it back. "I am not so easily won by bread that is hard and overdone," she chanted, before running back into the lake.

The next day, the shepherd returned to the lake. This time, he made sure that his bread was softer. He held his breath, fearful that the maidens would not reappear. But when the sun was high in the sky, they once again rose from the still water. And once again, the shepherd offered his bread to the one he loved.

It was no good. The girl's laughter rippled through the air as she ran back toward the lake. "Even less can I be won by bread so soft and underdone," she sang.

The shepherd did not know what else to do. The following day, as he stood by the lake shore, gazing out at the glossy surface, he noticed the bread that the maiden had dropped floating in the water. When she appeared once more, it was this that he offered her, with little hope in his heart.

To the shepherd's surprise, the maiden ate the bread with pleasure. Then she smiled at him. "I come to you as one of three. I will be yours if you know which is me."

Next day, the sunlight dazzled the shepherd as he gazed across the lake. The three maidens were all equally beautiful. But the shepherd had noticed that the straps of his chosen one's sandal bore a special design. He picked her out without hesitation.

"I will be your wife," said the girl gravely, "but if you raise your hand to me three times, I will be gone."

"I would never, ever harm you," cried the shepherd, and he meant it with all his being.

Then the lady called from the lake a small herd of six fine cattle and followed the shepherd to his home.

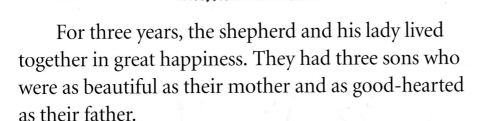

For three years, the shepherd and his lady lived together in great happiness. They had three sons who were as beautiful as their mother and as good-hearted as their father.

One day, the family was invited to a baptism.

"It is too far to walk," said the shepherd's wife. "I will harness the horses if you collect my cloak and gloves from the house."

The shepherd hurried away and soon returned, but he found to his surprise that his wife had not fetched the horses but was gazing out toward the hills, in a world of her own.

He tapped her playfully on the shoulder. "We must hurry," he said.

But the lady turned to her husband and looked deep into his eyes. "That was the first time," she said, with sorrow in her voice.

Some time later, the shepherd and his wife went to a wedding. All around them, people were laughing and dancing, but the lady from the lake suddenly fell to her knees, with tears running down her face.

The shepherd patted her on the back. "Why are you crying?" he asked.

"For the trouble that has come," replied his lady. "Now you have struck me twice. Take care. Next time will be the last time."

After that, the shepherd was careful never to raise his hand to his wife. Then, one day, the pair attended a funeral. As the coffin was carried past the white-faced mourners, the lady from the lake suddenly burst out laughing. It was so sudden and so strange that the shepherd grasped her roughly by the arm and begged her to stop.

"I was laughing for joy because the dead have no more sorrow," she said. "But your sorrow has just begun. You have struck me for the last time. Goodbye."

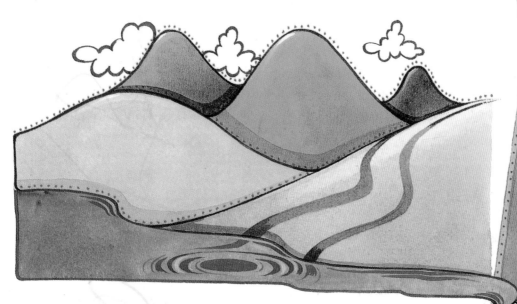

The lady walked off toward the lake, and as she went she called to her the cattle that she brought to the marriage. The oxen were at work in a field, but they followed her just the same, dragging the harrow behind them. You can see the mark that it made across the hills to this day.

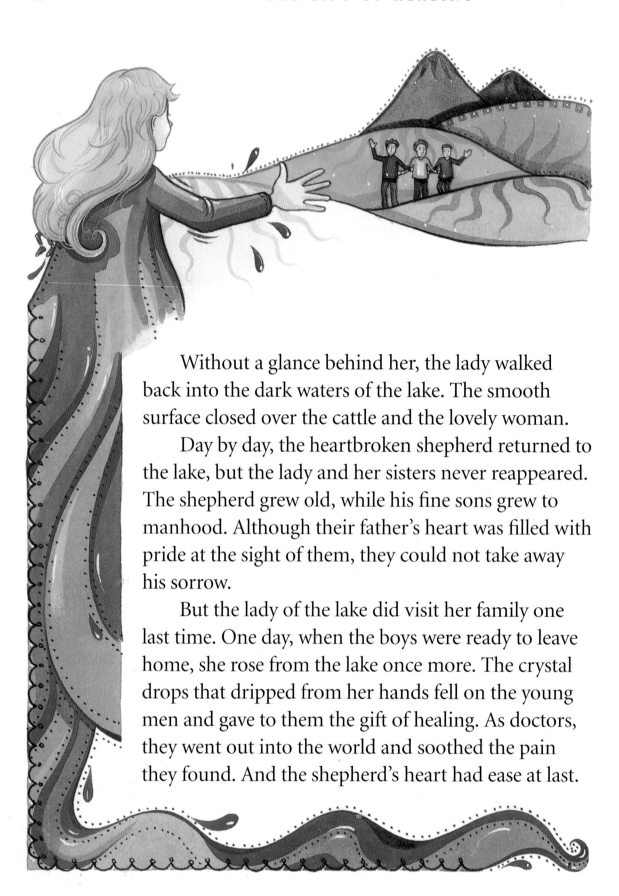

Without a glance behind her, the lady walked back into the dark waters of the lake. The smooth surface closed over the cattle and the lovely woman.

Day by day, the heartbroken shepherd returned to the lake, but the lady and her sisters never reappeared. The shepherd grew old, while his fine sons grew to manhood. Although their father's heart was filled with pride at the sight of them, they could not take away his sorrow.

But the lady of the lake did visit her family one last time. One day, when the boys were ready to leave home, she rose from the lake once more. The crystal drops that dripped from her hands fell on the young men and gave to them the gift of healing. As doctors, they went out into the world and soothed the pain they found. And the shepherd's heart had ease at last.